SHREK 2

Shrek

Donkey

Fiona

King Harold

Queen Lillian

Puss In Boots

The Fairy
Godmother

Prince
Charming

Once upon a time, in a smelly **swamp**, two happy **ogres**, Shrek and Fiona, returned from their honeymoon. Waiting for them was a special **invitation** from Fiona's parents, the King and Queen.

"We're going to a **royal** ball to celebrate our marriage!" Fiona shouted happily.

"I don't think that's such a good idea," sighed Shrek.

GO

Upon seeing Shrek and Fiona, the King and Queen were **shocked** that their daughter was still an ogress and that she had married an ogre as well!

"He's no Prince Charming!" thought the King as he eyed Shrek.

they're

mustn't

can't

weren't

haven't

don't

we'll

you've

it's

I'm

you'll

couldn't

At the royal dinner, it wasn't long before Shrek and the King forgot their manners. They began to **argue** and soon food was flying everywhere!

Fiona was sad that the **reunion** with her parents didn't go well. Suddenly, a large bubble floated into her bedroom and the Fairy Godmother appeared.

"With a wave of my magic **wand**, your troubles will soon be gone!"

thrown

where

roll

close

knight

waist

throne

scent

wear

role

Later that night, the Fairy Godmother **demanded** that the King get rid of Shrek.

"My son, Prince Charming, should have been the one to marry Fiona!" she **shrieked**.

waste

night

clothes

cent

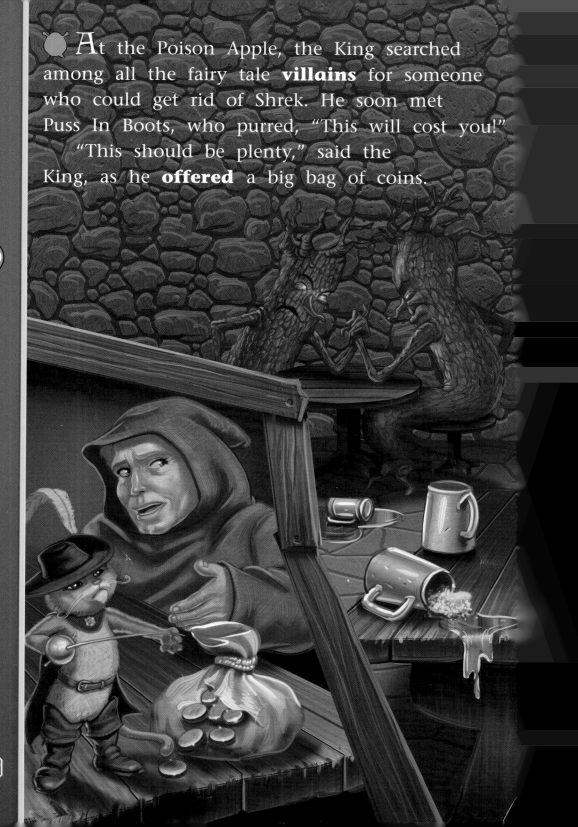

At the Poison Apple, the King searched among all the fairy tale **villains** for someone who could get rid of Shrek. He soon met Puss In Boots, who purred, "This will cost you!"

"This should be plenty," said the King, as he **offered** a big bag of coins.

"Where will I find Shrek?" hissed Puss. To **complete** his **wicked** plan, the King decided to invite Shrek to go hunting in the woods with him.

Pickled Eyeballs

ache
air
back
basket
ball
eye
fire
head
light
mail
horse
man
snow
tooth

Shrek

should

Donkey

Puss In
Boots

will

may

Wild Card!

must

can

GO

STOP

As he walked through the woods, Shrek heard an awful "HISSSSSS!" Suddenly, Puss **pounced** on Shrek! But Puss was no match for an ogre and he soon begged Shrek for **mercy**. "Please, señor! I will help you if you spare my life!" **pleaded** Puss.

scare

a hair ball

scratch

the birds

kiss

tickle

the rocks

the sword

Puss **revealed** that the King had hired him to attack Shrek. Hearing this, Shrek agreed to let Puss join him and Donkey.

"Maybe the Fairy Godmother could make me into a **handsome** prince," Shrek thought. "Let's pay her a visit!"

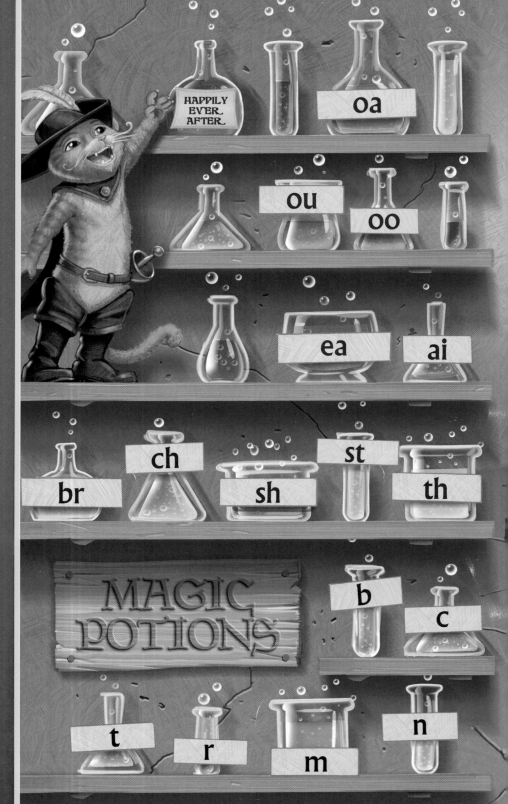

GO

STOP

12

Shrek asked the Fairy Godmother for help, but she refused.

"You see, ogres don't live happily ever after," she **warned**.

Still wanting to become a prince, Shrek took a Happily Ever After **potion** from her factory. Fighting off her guard elves, Shrek, Donkey, and Puss made a **daring escape**!

After drinking the potion, Shrek turned into a prince and Donkey a **noble steed**!

"I can **trot**! I can trot!" shouted Donkey.

Meanwhile, Puss learned that whoever takes the potion must kiss his true love by midnight to make the magic last. Back at the **castle**, Fiona found that she had become a beautiful princess!

use

appear

un

re

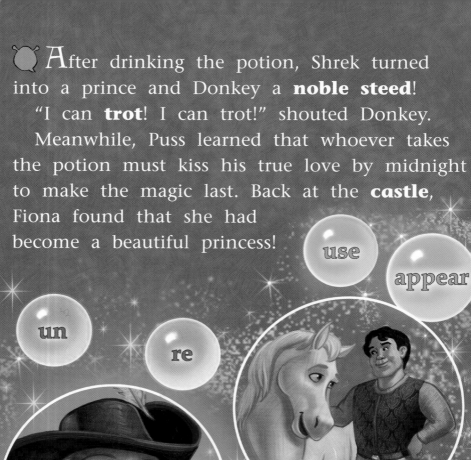

agree

Root Words

fear

hope

dis

power

Prefixes

GO

load

fold

Suffixes

ful

able

less

Now, the Fairy Godmother had to act fast! Fiona was tricked into thinking Prince Charming was really Shrek. Then, the Fairy Godmother **convinced** Shrek that he would never be right for Fiona.

"Deep down you will always be an ogre," she told him.

Sadly, Shrek decided it would be best to return to the swamp.

Before Shrek could return to the swamp, he and his pals were arrested and thrown into a **prison**. After seeing this on their Magic Mirror, Pinocchio and the fairy tale **characters** decided to save the day.

"Gingy! Pinocchio! Get us out of here!" cried Shrek.

With the help of Pinocchio's nose, they escaped and made their way to the castle.

"HA, HA! Now to **rescue** the fair Princess Fiona!" shouted Puss.

fix

polite

beautiful

stale

small

break

fast

rude

ugly

large

fresh

slow

dark

bright

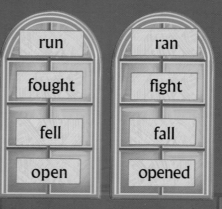

They all	run	ran	into the castle.
Puss and Shrek	fought	fight	the guards.
The guards	fell	fall	from the wall.
Shrek and Puss	open	opened	the door.

Shrek **burst** into the ball as Prince Charming **whirled** Fiona around the dance floor.

"Stay away from Fiona!" roared Shrek.

In a **tense** moment, Fiona realized that Prince Charming wasn't Shrek at all.

They all [rode] [ride] into the ball.

Fiona and the Prince [stop] [stopped] dancing.

Shrek [yells] [yelled] "stop!"

Everyone [looked] [looks] at Fiona.

present
tense

garlic

magical

frightening

transform

gingerbread

mushroom

Angry that Shrek had **ruined** everything, the Fairy Godmother **challenged** him to a battle.

"You couldn't just go back to the swamp and leave well enough alone!" she **bellowed**.

GO

STOP

mermaid

basketball

banister

window

balcony

Soaring into the air, she let her evil magic fly!

The King **leapt** in front of Shrek to block a big, magic blast that was about to hit him. Zing! The wicked magic bounced off the King's **armor** and right back to the Fairy Godmother!

"Oh poop," she squeaked, as she disappeared into a puff of smoke.

"Ribbit!" To everyone's surprise, the magic blast had turned the King into a frog!

"I'm sorry for all I've done," said the King.

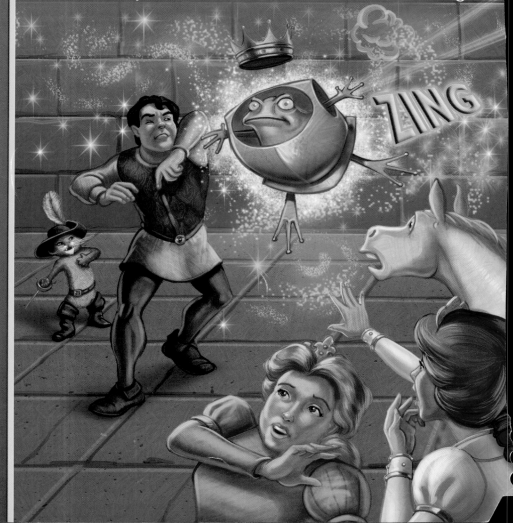

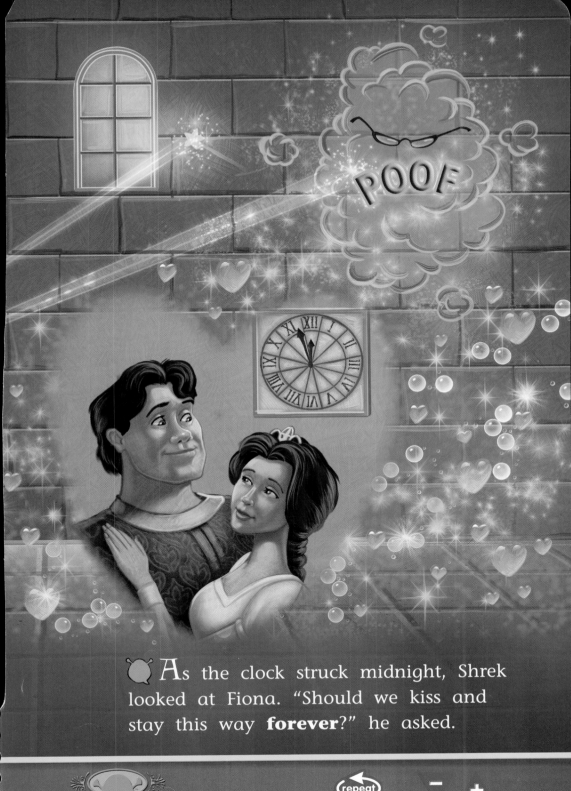

As the clock struck midnight, Shrek looked at Fiona. "Should we kiss and stay this way **forever**?" he asked.

"I'm happy with the man I married!" said Fiona.

Whoosh! She and Shrek were **transformed** back into ogres! Everyone began to sing and dance with joy. And that's how they all lived happily ever after... this time!

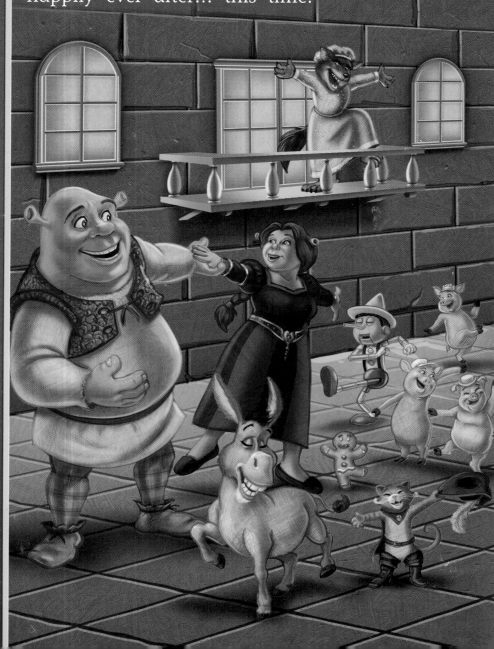

FAIRY TALE CHALLENGE

A SNEAK PEAK...

DARE YOUR MOM TO TOUCH HERE!

BEWARE!

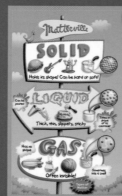

Actual book covers may vary.
Not all books are available in all markets.

26

CHECK OUT
THE ENTIRE LIBRARY AT
WWW.LEAPFROG.COM
TO FIND THE PERFECT BOOK!

Check out these other
LeapPad™ books
for 2nd Grade!

2nd Grade

Based on Dr. Seuss characters™ &
© Dr. Seuss Enterprises

TM & © Hanna-Barbera
TM & © Cartoon Network (s02)

TM & © Hanna-Barbera.
TM & © Cartoon Network (s02)

© 2001 Disney/Pixar

Created by Stephen Hillenburg

The LeapPad Library
includes over 60 books from
Pre-K to 5th Grade!
Visit **www.leapfrog.com** to learn more!

Not all books are
available in all markets.
Actual covers may vary.